2

Lies Over the Ocean

A Twentieth-Century One-Act "Odyssey"

by Lowery Christopher Collins

Lies Over the Ocean

A Twentieth-Century One-Act "Odyssey"

by Lowery Christopher Collins

Ponderlake Publishing

name of the author must appear on a separate line in which on other name appears, immediately beneath the title and in size and type equal to 50% of the size of the largest, most prominent letter used for the title of the play. No person, firm, or entity may receive credit larger or more prominent than that accorded the author.

LIES OVER THE OCEAN,
A TWENTIETH-CENTURY ONE-ACT "ODYSSEY"

Written by Lowery Christopher Collins

Ponderlake Publishing: www.ponderlake.com

Playwright and/or Royalty Information: www.ChristopherCollinsOnline.com

ISBN 978-1-7349926-0-1

Lies Over the Ocean

by Lowery Christopher Collins

CAST OF CHARACTERS

MCBRIDE ANDERSON

RICK BILLINGSLEY

PERIMETER

EDGAR

JACK

POLLY

CAROLINE BILLINGSLEY

BONNIE ANDERSON

SOPHIE DRUMMOND

IDIZOMARZA *(Eh-DEEZ-o-MAR-za)*

KATE

NORMA

CHILD'S VOICE

VARIOUS PARTYGOERS and CHORUS MEMBERS

Lies Over the Ocean

In the darkness, we hear strange, surrealistic music and the sounds of the ocean. We can barely make out random figures on stage. They are dressed in dark color. If there is any illumination of them at all, it is faint. Perhaps they have candles. Perhaps the lights are extremely low. Perhaps there is some sort of low-key lighting in their costumes. In the darkness we hear them speak.

CHORUS 1. Homer. (*Beat*) *From* The Odyssey, Book 9—

CHORUS 2. We hear the words of Odysseus.

CHORUS 3. *We found ourselves at last in the land of the Lotus-eaters.*

CHORUS 4. These folks are harmless enough, but the plant on which they feast is insidious.

CHORUS 3. Three of my men tasted it and all they wanted was more.

CHORUS 5. They lost all desire for home.

CHORUS 2. I had to force them back to the ships and tie them down while we made our getaway.

There is large crash of thunder and a flash of lightning. The scene changes and the energy level increases. The chorus members quickly interchange places with each other.

CHORUS 1. Later he visits Polyphemus in the Land of the Cyclops.

CHORUS 5. It turned out that the favor he intended was to eat me last. But when the wine had knocked him out, I put my plan into effect.

CHORUS 4. Heating the end of the pole until it was glowing red, we ran it toward the Cyclops like a battering ram, aiming it for his eye and driving it deep.

CHORUS 3. The thing sizzled like hot metal dropped in water while I twisted it like an auger.

CHORUS 2. Polyphemus came awake with a roar, tore the spike from his eye and began groping for us in his blindness.

CHORUS 1. But that was long ago.

CHORUS 1 & 2.   But that was long ago.

ALL CHORUS MEMBERS.   But that was long ago.

CHORUS 3. And each person.

CHORUS 4. Each person.

CHORUS 5. Must distinguish truth from lies.

CHORUS 1. Lies.

CHORUS 2. Lies.

CHORUS 3. Lies.

CHORUS 1. And find out

CHORUS 3. What lies

CHORUS 2. What lies

ALL CHORUS MEMBERS.   LIES

CHORUS 1. Over the Ocean

ALL CHORUS MEMBERS. OVER THE OCEAN

The stage goes black. The chorus members exit. The loud roar of the ocean waves and a thunderstorm echo through the blackness as the sounds of violent hurricane permeate the entire room.
During the course of the storm and the lines, a few lightning flashes occur, showing quick glimpses of something dark on stage.

VOICE OF CHILD.   Momma! Momma!

BONNIE'S VOICE.   It's okay, sweetheart. You're safe. You're here with me.

VOICE OF CHILD.   Momma, I'm scared.

BONNIE'S VOICE.   I know, baby. It's all right if you're scared.

VOICE OF CHILD.   Is the hurricane going to kill us?

BONNIE'S VOICE.   No, sweetheart. We're going to be fine. We're going to be fine. Hold on!

The winds get louder. The rain gets louder.

The sound of a song soars over the hurricane.

OFFSTAGE VOICES.   *(Singing)* My Bonnie lies over the ocean. My Bonnie lies over the sea. My Bonnie lies over the ocean. Oh, bring back my Bonnie to me.

MCBRIDE.   *(Singing, loudly, by himself, in the darkness)* Bring back my Bonnie to me.

The lights come up on a man lying on the floor. He is restless, obviously experiencing turmoil in his sleep. His name is MCBRIDE; he speaks with a Scottish dialect.

RICK enters. The hurricane tech elements stop abruptly. Lights come up to (approximately) 50%--giving the illusion of nighttime. Rick is an American.

RICK.   McBride! McBride. Wake up, man.

MCBRIDE.	*(waking up)* Wha . . .? Wha . . . 'tis . . .
RICK.	McBride! Wake up. You're dreaming again.
MCBRIDE.	I'm what? Oh. *(Becoming more cognizant.)*
RICK.	I understand. You can't help it, but you're waking up my kids again. *(Smiles, obviously NOT upset with McBride)*
MCBRIDE.	I'm sorry, Rick. I'll try to be quiet the rest of the night. I'll not be attempting to sleep again this eve.
RICK.	I'm not suggesting that you *not* sleep.
MCBRIDE.	It's not a suggestion. Aye. I know. It's a subtle request.
RICK.	I'm sorry, McBride.
MCBRIDE.	*(getting a towel or washcloth and washing his face.)* No need for apologies. You have small children. They need their beauty rest. And I'm a burden.
RICK.	*(Interrupting)* No, you're not. Listen. I can take them out this morning, maybe to get some ice cream, get some alcohol, go to the shooting range or something so you can get some rest. Maybe, we can give you a few hours of sleep.
MCBRIDE.	No. You go about your life. Don't mind me at all. This is your house, and you're kind enough to let me stay here a few days.
RICK.	McBride . . .
MCBRIDE.	Rick. I'm okay. Really.
RICK.	The hurricane again?
MCBRIDE.	*(Uncomfortable pause)* Aye.
RICK.	The child?
MCBRIDE.	*(hesitating)* Aye.

16

RICK.	I wish there were something I could do to help you.
MCBRIDE.	You've helped me more than you'll ever know.
RICK.	Eh. It's a just a bed.
MCBRIDE.	And a warm, dry place. And food.
RICK.	It's nothing.
MCBRIDE.	It's ever'thin'. *(Beat.)* But it can't last forever.
RICK.	It's just a bed. You . . . saved my life.
MCBRIDE.	And you've saved mine. *(Beat.)* More than once.
RICK.	I'm not keeping score.
MCBRIDE.	'Course not. Life's too complicated for that. I'll be gone soon. I just have to figure out where to find her.

Caroline, Rick's wife, walks in. It's obvious that she is exhausted.

CAROLINE.	Everything okay?
RICK.	Yeah.
MCBRIDE.	Sorry I woke the girls.
CAROLINE.	They're asleep again. All's well.

Caroline, sleepily, grabs Rick's arm and puts her head on his shoulder.

MCBRIDE.	All's well.
CAROLINE.	Are you having the nightmares again?
MCBRIDE.	It's nothin'.
CAROLINE.	It's more than nothing.

MCBRIDE laughs out loud. CAROLINE, leans up, and joins in involuntary sympathetic laughter. RICK smiles and looks at CAROLINE, then looks back to MCBRIDE.

RICK.	What's so funny?
MCBRIDE.	It's just what Caroline said.
CAROLINE.	"It's more than nothing"?
MCBRIDE.	Sounds like what my mum used to say. At least once a day, she'd say . . .

Across the stage, the lights come up on BONNIE, standing, looking over the audience. She is a young woman, also with a Scottish brogue. As the lights come up on BONNIE, they fade on the previous trio of actors, but keeping one downstage area for MCBRIDE to walk into, as he has a conversation with BONNIE, over the audience.

BONNIE.	Anythin' is better than nothin'!
MCBRIDE.	I ain't . . .
BONNIE.	(*Interrupting*) You're NOT.
MCBRIDE.	What?
BONNIE.	What?! "Ma'am."
MCBRIDE.	(*Realizing that he should have been more respectful in his response*) Ma'am.
BONNIE.	You're NOT. Don't use "ain't." It's common. And you're not common.
MCBRIDE.	(*tired of the conversation*) Aye.
BONNIE.	What?!
MCBRIDE.	Yes, ma'am.
BONNIE.	Now, my boy, my little man, what were you sayin'?
MCBRIDE.	You said that anythin' is better than nothin'.
BONNIE.	Indeed, I did. Because 'tis true. (*Beat.*) As gospel. Aye.
MCBRIDE.	But I'm trying . . .

BONNIE.	No, you're trying at trying. I don't abide laziness and half-hearted living in my household. You're my son, McBride. You have the blood of the Andersons, the Gibsons, and the Wallaces flowing through your veins. But most of all, you have McBride blood in you. Whatever other mutts are in there, we can't help. We focus on the good.
MCBRIDE.	Yes, ma'am.
BONNIE.	Life is for the living! We don't rest. If it takes working ourselves to the bone, we do it. Death waits for no man, so we outrun it!
MCBRIDE.	(softly) Even the winds of death.
BONNIE.	What'd you say?
MCBRIDE.	Nothing, Mum.
BONNIE.	What did you say?
MCBRIDE.	I've been having dreams again. It's the storm . . .
BONNIE.	Enough of that. You need to start getting to bed earlier, quit reading those foolish books.
MCBRIDE.	But it's . . .
BONNIE.	I know exactly what it is, and it's something you stop. You stop it. (Beat.) You.
MCBRIDE.	Aye.
BONNIE.	There's a storm *inside* of you, my boy. You have to get it out of your soul. It's messing with your thinking. Fix it. (Beat) You.
MCBRIDE.	Aye.
BONNIE.	From the bottom of my being, I love you, McBride. You're my heart and mind. You're my very blood.
MCBRIDE.	I love you, too.

The lights fade on BONNIE as they come up on SOPHIE, also Scottish. The lights stay up on MCBRIDE.

SOPHIE.   So, you're not ashamed to say that *back* to a girl then?

MCBRIDE.   *(caught off-guard)* What?

SOPHIE.   Was it so traumatic that you don't remember that you just told me that you love me, too, McBride Anderson?

MCBRIDE.   What?

SOPHIE.   *(smiling)* Quit "whatting" me, you big coward. You just told me that you loved me, too.

MCBRIDE.   Yes, I do. Of course.

SOPHIE.   Unless you didn't mean it?

MCBRIDE.   I don't say things I don't mean.

SOPHIE.   So, your mum raised you well, then?

MCBRIDE.   You could say that.

SOPHIE.   Is everything okay? You've just drifted from me. What happened?

MCBRIDE.   Nothin'. Nothin' at all. Sophie, I told you I love you, and I mean it. Don't be doubtin' my words.

SOPHIE.   Look at ye. Talkin' all manly. You don' fool me, McBride. You're a soft and gentle as a newborn kitten, ye are!

MCBRIDE.   Are ye sure, you're not mistakin' me for Byron Manning?

SOPHIE.   Are you out of your head, you daft man? Byron Manning. I never once showed him the time of day.

MCBRIDE.   He sure watched your clock, though.

20

SOPHIE.	He can watch as long as I don't catch 'im. But he canno' touch. I only have eyes for you, my boy. You're the only man in all o' Scotland for me.
MCBRIDE.	Is that supposed to make me feel special, Sophie Drummond?
SOPHIE.	You better hush your mouth 'fore I smack you across it!

Lighting flashes and thunder roars. McBride notices the storm, but Sophie does not. We hear a child crying. A light appears on stage down center. McBride walks into the light. The lights on Sophie, who is now alone, fades to black.

OFFSTAGE VOICE.	(*Singing*) My Bonnie lies over the ocean.
MCBRIDE.	(*Singing*) Oh, bring back my Bonnie to me.

The lights pop back to levels of the earlier scene with Rick and Caroline. To Rick and Caroline, no time has passed.

CAROLINE.	What'd she say?
MCBRIDE.	(*Confused*) What?
CAROLINE.	You said she told you something once per day.
MCBRIDE.	Oh. I . . .
RICK.	You need some sleep, my friend.
CAROLINE.	We all do. It's late. Let's call it a night . . . again.

There is a loud knocking at the door. The sounds of girls crying and calling out for "Mommy."

RICK.	You gotta be kiddin' me.
CAROLINE.	I'll tend to them. Go see who that is. (*Beat*) For the love of all things holy!
RICK.	I'll see.

Caroline and Rick leave the stage in frenzy. As soon as they leave, MCBRIDE sees lightning and hears thunder. He looks around for the source. After a few seconds, RICK reenters. The lightning and thunder stop. RICK stops.

RICK.	You okay?
MCBRIDE.	Yeah, I'm fine.
RICK.	You've got company.
MCBRIDE.	What? Me? Now?
RICK.	You. Now. In the middle of the night.

A man in a tuxedo enters. He is suave and confident. His name is PERIMETER. He has a strong French accent.

PERIMETER.	Bonjour, Mr. Anderson. My name is Pe-ree-muh-TEEEHRR.
MCBRIDE.	Pe-ree-muh-TEEEHRR?
PERIMETER.	Pe-ree-muh-TEEEHRR, like the outer distance of a geometric figure.
MCBRIDE.	Perimeter?
RICK.	I think he means perimeter.
PERIMETER.	*Oui*. I mean, yes, Pe-ree-muh-TEEEHRR. Okay. Perimeter if that helps you.
MCBRIDE.	Excuse my bluntness, but who are you? Why are you looking for me? And why are you here at such an ungodly hour?
PERIMETER.	So many questions. I apologize. I wasn't aware of the hour. I don't sleep. Ever. Sleep is for the weak and the boring.
MCBRIDE.	Why are you here? How do you know me?
PERIMETER.	Mr. Anderson, I rather *sus*pected that you would be *ex*pecting me.
MCBRIDE.	Wait. Do you have news on . . .
PERIMETER.	Ms. Drummond, *oui*.

22

MCBRIDE.	(*moving toward Perimeter*) What do you know? Where is she?
PERIMETER.	I don't know exactly where she is, but I do know someone who wants to see you.
MCBRIDE.	I'm not playing any more games. I came to America because that's where they told she is. I'm waited and waited, and I am not dealing with the policemen any more.
PERIMETER.	Mr. Anderson, I don't work with the police. And you know that. And you know that the one who wants to see you is not with the police.
MCBRIDE.	Who is it?
PERIMETER.	Her name is Idizomarza.
MCBRIDE.	Idizomarza?
RICK.	I've heard of her.
MCBRIDE and PERIMETER.	You have?
RICK.	Yeah. The guys down at the dock have mentioned her. She's crazy. Bad news. She's showed up a few times starting about three weeks ago. Things happen to people who talk with her.
PERIMETER.	My demise is soon then. For she sought me out. She told me that I was looking to help you.
MCBRIDE.	But I don't know you.
PERIMETER.	It does not matter. I was following a request.
RICK.	McBride, what's all this about?
MCBRIDE.	I have to go see this Idizomarza.
RICK.	No way, man.
MCBRIDE.	I have to. If she has news about Sophie, I have to.
RICK.	Well, you ain't goin' by yourself.

MCBRIDE.	Rick.
RICK.	Don't argue with me. I'm going with you.
PERIMETER.	If so, you'd better go now. She's waiting for you by the bay, a hundred meters south of the McHenry dock in Newbury.
MCBRIDE.	Now?
PERIMETER.	Now.
RICK.	Well, let me tell Caroline. This'll top off her night.
PERIMETER.	I have lives to save, women to seduce. *Adieu*, gentlemen.

The lights fade on the Perimeter scene and come up on a darkened bay scene.

We hear the sound of water hitting the shore. We see an odd woman dressed in many layers. She is IDIZOMARZA and speaks with a strong Italian accent.

MCBRIDE and RICK approach her.

MCBRIDE.	There she is.
RICK.	Just as I figured.
IDIZOMARZA.	What did you figure, Rick Billingsley?
RICK.	Wait a minute! How . . .?
IDIZOMARZA.	I see that you received my message, Julian McBride Anderson.
MCBRIDE.	Well, I *am* here I suppose. What information do you have for me?
IDIZOMARZA.	So quick. So to-the-point. We haven't even had a chance to speak, Julian McBride Anderson.
MCBRIDE.	"McBride" is good enough.
IDIZOMARZA.	I know, Julian McBride Anderson, but I don't live by your rules.

RICK.	Are you going to help him or not?
IDIZOMARZA.	Are *you*?
RICK.	What?
IDIZOMARZA.	Are you going to help do what has to be done? Assist him with the major task before him? Go with him to find that which he seeks?
RICK.	Sure. I'm here, aren't I?
IDIZOMARZA.	This is one mere step on a journey of thousands.
MCBRIDE.	This is my task, not his. I have to find Sophie. She's my only link.
IDIZOMARZA.	If you only knew the truth of your statement!
RICK.	Whatever this is, you're not doing it alone.
IDIZOMARZA.	It's a sizable undertaking.
MCBRIDE.	You have a wife and daughter at home . . .
RICK.	. . . who will understand.
IDIZOMARZA.	It seems you have a friend for the journey, Julian McBride Anderson.
MCBRIDE.	What can you . . .
IDIZOMARZA.	You went to war. You fought in many battles. There you met Rick Eugene Billingsley.
RICK.	No need to get nasty.
IDIZOMARZA.	A son of the Isles and a son of the cousins fighting side-by-side. And then when it came time to go home . . .
MCBRIDE.	How do you know all this?
IDIZOMARZA.	You found your mother had passed, the fair, out-spoken Bonnie.

MCBRIDE.	Please don't.
IDIZOMARZA.	(*quickly*) And your one true love was gone.
MCBRIDE.	Where is she?
IDIZOMARZA.	(*Ignoring him*) She was gone, Julian McBride Anderson. Thinking you dead, she left for America.
RICK.	Thinking you dead?
IDIZOMARZA.	Si, she left for America.
MCBRIDE.	(*emotionally*) Or she was taken.
IDIZOMARZA.	Or . . . she was taken.
RICK.	Taken?
MCBRIDE.	She WAS taken!
IDIZOMARZA.	Or she wasn't.
MCBRIDE.	She WAS. Where is she?
IDIZOMARZA.	You don't want to find her.
MCBRIDE.	Where is she?
IDIZOMARZA.	This isn't just the fifth week in 1947.
RICK.	What?
IDIZOMARZA.	All roads have led to this week. (*During the course of her words, we hear the sounds of battle, gun fire, men yelling, and we see flashing lights, symbolic of gunshots and war. MCBRIDE and RICK both see and hear the war memories and are not only surprised at the lights and sounds, but also surprised to notice that the other person can also sense these lights and sounds.*) Three years ago, Julian McBride Anderson, Rick Eugene Billingsley saved your life in battle in northern France. (*We hear Rick's voice screaming, "McBride!" Fearfully, as if he'd never actually heard this yelling before, he stares wide-eyed at Rick.*)

RICK.   What?

IDIZOMARZA.   1944. France. War. Gunfire. A shot. Blood. A
                         tourniquet. A friendship. *(The war sounds stop.)* But
                         going back seven years, back to the Isles.

MCBRIDE.   Stop.

IDIZOMARZA.   Promises. Goodbyes. *(The sounds of ocean
                         waves/water whipping up on the beach and dim lights
                         begin as we hear the voice of Bonnie saying, "Don't
                         you be worrying about me, my handsome man of a
                         boy. You go do what you have to." We hear McBride's
                         voice: "Momma, you're sick. I can't leave you like
                         this," followed by Bonnie: "You have to, McBride.
                         This is war. You have no choice." Immediately, we
                         hear the voice of Sophie: "I'll be waiting for you, my
                         lover boy. You come home a hero, and I'll be right
                         here on the beach.")*

RICK.   What is this?

IDIZOMARZA.   Beware, Julian McBride Anderson. Do not seek that
                         which you think you want. This is a warning.

MCBRIDE.   Where is she, Idizomarza?

As the lights flash, we hear McBride's voice come from offstage: "Where is she?"

We then see a woman, shadows, downstage left, standing, appearing distraught.

We hear McBride's voice again: "Where is she? She told me she'd wait on me."

The WOMAN IN SHADOWS responds.

WOMAN.   She waited. She waited. She came to the beach
                         every morning and every evening, waiting on you. But
                         . . . but . . .

MCBRIDE's VOICE.   But what?

MCBRIDE.   But what?

WOMAN.   She was taken. I don't think it was her will. It couldn't
                         have been. She was taken.

27

MCBRIDE's VOICE.	Taken?
MCBRIDE.	Taken.
WOMAN.	Aye, taken. I know my own baby girl. She was taken. (*She exits.*)
MCBRIDE.	She was taken.

The lights change, shifting to the side.

IDIZOMARZA.	Taken. Taken away . . .

The voice of another woman, McBride's aunt, is heard offstage.

AUNT'S VOICE.	McBride, my handsome nephew, oh, McBride, you're alive. I'm so happy you made it home.
MCBRIDE'S VOICE.	Auntie, thank you. Where's my mother?
AUNT'S VOICE.	Oh, McBride. She . . . Your mom, my dear sister . . .
MCBRIDE'S VOICE.	Oh, no.
AUNT'S VOICE.	I'm so, sorry, McBride. She tried to hold on until you returned to Scotland, but she was too sick.
MCBRIDE.	Stop!

The lights change.

IDIZOMARZA.	Your sweet momma and your sweet Sophie. To come home and find them both gone. The ones waiting on you. And Sophie just up and gone.
RICK.	McBride . . .
MCBRIDE.	I've lost everything. Where is she, Idizomarza?
IDIZOMARZA.	Are you making a choice?
MCBRIDE.	Where is she?
IDIZOMARZA.	You've been warned. Prepare for your journey.

RICK.	McBride.
MCBRIDE.	Go home, Rick. I have to do this.
IDIZOMARZA.	Going to face the journey alone?
RICK.	No.
MCBRIDE.	Go home.
RICK.	You're not doing this alone. I won't allow it.
MCBRIDE.	You have a family . . .
RICK and IDIZOMARZA.	. . . who'll understand.
RICK.	. . . who'll understand.
MCBRIDE.	(*Sighs.*) Where is she?
IDIZOMARZA.	Look! (*She points to a bottle on stage. A light comes up on the area. As McBride and Rick turn their attention to the bottle, Idizomarza exits.*)
MCBRIDE.	(*Picking up the bottle*) What's this, Idiz . . . Where'd she go?
RICK.	I don't know.
MCBRIDE.	Idizomarza!
RICK.	What's on the bottle?
MCBRIDE.	What?
RICK.	What's written on the bottle?
MCBRIDE.	(*Reading*) 100% American Whiskey. (*Pause*) Sophie's Finest.
RICK.	What else?

McBride, confused, hands Rick the bottle.

RICK.	(*Continuing to read*) Matured in the Berkshire Mountains, at Madison Gorge, Massachusetts.

MCBRIDE.	Madison Gorge.
RICK.	Wait. I know where that is.
MCBRIDE.	Good. Come on.

They exit.

The sounds of rural mountain music, circa 1947, begins. The scene transitions to a dance. Several people are laughing, talking, eating, drinking, and dancing. McBride and Rick enter.

MCBRIDE.	Is this it?
RICK.	This is where the guy at the coffee shop said that the whiskey is made.
MCBRIDE.	Are they in a continual party?
RICK.	We may be, too, if we made whiskey for a living.

A young woman approaches. Her name is Katherine.

KATE.	Well, hello. I've never seen you two here before.
MCBRIDE.	We're just visiting.
KATE.	Ah.
RICK.	Does this go on every night?
KATE.	This? The dancing? No, this is a special occasion. The drinking? That's another story. (*She laughs.*)
MCBRIDE.	A special occasion?
KATE.	We have a special guest with us tonight, and we wanted to give him our friendliest welcome. (*Beat*) But it looks like we have a couple more guests. (*Pause*) I'm Katherine Connor. But friends call me Kate.
RICK.	It's a pleasure, Katherine. I'm Rick, and this is McBride.

KATE.	Call me Kate. I make friends fast. And McBride. What a name. Are you British or something?
MCBRIDE.	I'm from Scotland. (*Quickly*) Has anything usual happened around here recently?
KATE.	(*Laughing at the turn of conversation*) Aren't *you* two the serious types? Everything that happens around here is unusual. This is Madison Gorge, the strangest town in the Berkshires, maybe in all of Massachusetts, with the exception of Salem, that is. (*She laughs yet again.*)
MCBRIDE.	Have you seen a young woman? Has a young woman shown up recently?
KATE.	(*Thinking*) A young woman?
MCBRIDE.	About yea tall. (*He indicates a certain height.*) Also Scottish?
KATE.	If another Scotland person showed up, I'd have known it.
MCBRIDE.	Her name is Sophie.
KATE.	(*Grinning*) Sophie? Are you pulling my leg?
RICK.	What?
KATE.	This is a joke. This is Madison Gorge. Haven't you looked around you? We MAKE Sophie's Finest Berkshire Whiskey. Did Ted put you up to this? This is crazy.
MCBRIDE.	I assure you: this is no joke. (*to Rick*) Perhaps we need to go looking around town.
KATE.	I wouldn't do that at night. People wouldn't like that. Don't go! Stay. Have a drink. Join us. We can ask around to see if anybody knows anything about a girl from Scotland, if this isn't a practical joke.

A young man walks up.

EDGAR.	What's going on, Katie? Who are these fine gentlemen?
KATE.	Don't call me Katie. This is McBride and . . . (*searching*)
RICK.	Rick.
KATE. EDGAR.	Right. Rick. Sorry. McBride and Rick. All right. Still a bit fuzzy. But hello, Rick. McBride.
KATE.	They're looking for a Sophie.
EDGAR.	We've got gallons and gallons of Sophie. (*He laughs.*)
KATE.	Not our Sophie. A girl named Sophie. From Scotland.
EDGAR.	Scotland? Nobody from Scotland's ever been to Madison Gorge.
KATE.	Until now. (*She points at McBride.*)
EDGAR.	What? Really? You're from Scotland?
MCBRIDE.	I am. (*to Rick*) We really don't have time for this. I've got to find Sophie.
EDGAR.	You're serious.
MCBRIDE.	Most serious. Unless we've been lead on a wild goose chase.
EDGAR.	Wait a minute. There's somebody I want you to meet. (*Steps away quickly*)
MCBRIDE.	Let's get out of here, Rick. There are no answers here.
KATE.	It's too late at night for conversation, boys. Let's laugh and dance.

Edgar returns with a special guest.

EDGAR.	Jack, I'd like to introduce you to a couple of guests who just showed up at our little soirée. This is Rick and McBride. McBride is straight from Scotland.
JACK.	Ah, Scotland.
EDGAR.	Gentlemen, this is Jack Kennedy from over in Boston. He was just elected to Congress, down in Washington. He was visiting over in this part of the state, so we threw him this little shindig.
JACK.	It's nice to meet you.
RICK.	Nice to meet you, too, Mr. Kennedy. Sorry. I don't keep up with politics.
JACK.	I envy you. I wish I didn't have to. And call me Jack, please. Mr. Kennedy is my father. (*Beat, then to McBride*) From Scotland?
MCBRIDE.	Aye.
JACK.	Most of my family came from right across the sea there in Ireland.
MCBRIDE.	(*Not very interested*) I won't hold it against you.
RICK.	His mind is elsewhere.
MCBRIDE.	As yours should be. We're not here to socialize.
KATE.	But this is a party!
JACK.	Are you on a mission or a journey of sorts?
RICK.	As a matter of fact . . .
MCBRIDE.	Aye, and this is a waste. It's a total sham.
EDGAR.	There's no need to be rude.
RICK.	He's not talking about your party. It's the . . . mission, as Jack put it.
MCBRIDE.	I should never have listened to that woman.

33

EDGAR.	Sophie?
RICK.	No.
MCBRIDE.	That slippery soothsayer.
JACK.	Soothsayer?
RICK.	It's a long story.
KATE.	And this is supposed to be a party!
MCBRIDE.	Bloody Idizomarza.
JACK.	What?
EDGAR.	What'd you say?
RICK.	That's just the name of the old woman who . . .
JACK.	Idizomarza. (*He looks at Edgar, who looks back with shock.*)
MCBRIDE.	Vixen from hell.
RICK.	Why are you . . .?
EDGAR.	Jack.
JACK.	A woman came in here earlier, before most people arrived. She looked a bit rough around the edges and started snooping around.
KATE.	Oh, that was the creepy woman!
JACK.	She kept telling us that she was Idizomarza and that she was looking for something. And she left . . . something.
MCBRIDE.	What? What'd she leave?
EDGAR.	I'll get it. (*He steps away.*)
KATE.	Are you sure you don't want to dance? (*to Rick*) You know, you're rather handsome.

JACK.	Kate, let's dance a bit later.
EDGAR.	(*Returning with a small toy ship*) Here.
JACK.	Wait. This Idizomarza woman sent you here? To this place.
MCBRIDE.	Aye. (*taking the toy from Edgar*) A toy?
RICK.	McBride, can I see that? Is it? (*Beat*) It is.
MCBRIDE.	What is it? Just a toy.
RICK.	It's the . . . S.S. Sophia Bella.
MCBRIDE.	What?
RICK.	The Sophia Bella. I know it.
MCBRIDE.	Where?
RICK.	In port. In Mystic.
JACK.	This boat? In Mystic now?
MCBRIDE.	Sophia.
RICK.	Is this some sort of game?
MCBRIDE.	Let's go.

McBride and Rick start to go.

JACK.	Wait.
MCBRIDE.	We have to go.
JACK.	I'm coming with you.
RICK.	What?
EDGAR.	What?
MCBRIDE.	No.

KATE.	But you're a Congressman. You're not a profile in courage.
EDGAR.	Katherine!
JACK.	I don't know why, but I need to come with you.
RICK.	You don't even know why we're looking.
JACK.	Explain it to me on the way.
MCBRIDE.	Look.
JACK.	Explain it to me on the way. (*Thunder cracks very loudly.*) The weather's bad, we have over 100 miles to cover to get to Mystic.
MCBRIDE.	Mr. Kennedy!
JACK.	It's Jack to my friends; remember? Come on!

At the lightning flashes and the thunder roars, Edgar stares as the three men exit.

KATE.	(*Yelling and laughing*) Dance, everybody. Dance like there's no tomorrow. There may not be.

During this transition, as the lights fade on the party, the lightning continues to flash. The music dies down from the shindig, and we hear voices singing, "My Bonnie lies over the ocean. My Bonnie lies over the sea." The lights come up on the bow a boat. It's the SS Sophia Bella. The singing fades. McBride, Rick, and Jack enter and approach the boat.

RICK.	That's it.
MCBRIDE.	The Sophia Bella.
JACK.	Could she be here?
MCBRIDE.	(*yells out*) Sophie!
JACK.	That's one way to find out.
RICK.	Let's see if anyone's onboard.

Rick, McBride, and Jack climb aboard the ship.

JACK.	How much boat experience have you had, Rick?
RICK.	Not as much as I should have. You?
JACK.	A bit in the war.
MCBRIDE.	Sophie!
RICK.	I don't think anyone's here.
MCBRIDE.	Sophie!
RICK.	Do we look below?
JACK.	This IS someone's boat. And we're trespassing. That may not look good for a Congressman.
MCBRIDE.	We all know how honest politicians are.
JACK.	Some of us try. And I'm new to this. It wasn't like it was my life dream or anything.
RICK.	What do you mean?
JACK.	It's a long story.
RICK.	No plans to be President then?
JACK.	Me? Not really? My father's plans for me? That's another story.
MCBRIDE.	Can we look for Sophie please?
JACK.	Of course.
RICK.	The wind's picking up.
JACK.	Sophie? Are you on here?
MCBRIDE.	I guess I fell for the old lady's lies again. (*He sits on the inside edge of the boat.*)
RICK.	(*Sitting down next to him*) We'll find her. She has to be somewhere, and this Idizomarza has some link.

JACK.	Gentlemen, I think we have a problem.
RICK.	What?
JACK.	We're no longer in port. We've moved out into the bay.
MCBRIDE.	Are you kidding me?
JACK.	What?

They frantically look around, over the boat, toward the shore.

MCBRIDE.	We have.
RICK.	How did this happen? I'm not a sailor. I hate the water.
JACK.	Calm down. We'll be okay.
RICK.	Okay? We're moving out to sea. We're just free-floating. In a storm. And . . . I . . . can't swim.
JACK.	It'll be okay. It's not quite a storm. Just a bit of wind and rain.
MCBRIDE.	I don't like this. Somet'in's not right here. In fact, . . . we're not alone.
RICK.	What?
JACK.	How do you know that?
MCBRIDE.	I just know.
RICK.	(*Yells*) Help!
MCBRIDE.	Rick!

The figure of a man appears in shadow.

MAN.	(*in a French accent*) I would not scream too loudly, Mr. Billingsley.
MCBRIDE.	Perimeter?!

JACK.	Perimeter?
RICK.	Wait a minute. (*Starting to get seasick*)
MCBRIDE.	What is this? What are you doing here?
PERIMETER.	Oh, Mr. Anderson. I'm surprised at your naiveté.
JACK.	What's going on?
MCBRIDE.	You have her? What have you done with her?

Jack starts to approach Perimeter. PERIMETER reveals that he has a revolver.

While he doesn't point it at the men, it makes sure they know that he has it.

PERIMETER.	No, no, no. I think you have this all wrong. I am not your enemy. I've here to help you.
RICK.	Help us? (*Rick is now obviously very seasick.*)
JACK.	Do you have the girl?
PERIMETER.	No, no, no! I'm trying to help you find the girl!
MCBRIDE.	By setting us out to sea in a storm?
RICK.	On a boat no one's sailing?
PERIMETER.	Everything is under control, gentleman. This is a not a real storm. And in any case, I have one of my men navigating everything for us.
JACK.	You have someone else on here?
RICK.	One of your men? You have men?
PERIMETER.	I have resources at my fingertips. It's amazing what association can do for you.
JACK.	And the girl?
PERIMETER.	I would calm down, Mr. Kennedy. I would hate to see what the press would do with a son of the

	ambassador trespassing and then stealing a boat out of a Connecticut bay.
JACK.	How do you know who . . . ?
PERIMETER.	Associations, Mr. Kennedy. Associations. Like I said, I'm here to help you, gentlemen. Sit down. Relax. I have it all covered. People are on board to get us where we're going.
RICK.	Where we're going?
MCBRIDE.	Where are we going? To Sophie?
PERIMETER.	Relax. Just rest.

A woman's voice echoes across stage with "Just rest. Sleep."

MCBRIDE, RICK, and JACK all slowly sit, relax, and go to sleep.

Transition music play as they arrive at their destination. The boat stops.

PERIMETER.	Wakey, wakey, gentlemen.

The three men stir to consciousness.

MCBRIDE.	Where are we?
JACK.	How long have we been out?
RICK.	We've stopped. Thank God.
JACK.	How long?
PERIMETER.	Just a bit of time. Does it matter? Two hours? Four?
JACK.	Hours??
MCBRIDE.	Where are we? Is she here?
PERIMETER.	Welcome to the island. *(to himself)* However do I get hired for this type of job? *(Back to the passengers)* Welcome to Cyclone Island.
JACK.	Cyclone Island? I've never heard of . . .

PERIMETER.	There are more things in heaven and earth, oui?
MCBRIDE.	(*Jumping off the boat.*) Sophie? Sophie!
PERIMETER.	You do follow your heart, don't you?
JACK.	Why have you brought us here?
RICK.	Where is this?

Jack and Rick exit the boat to join McBride. Perimeter stays on board.

PERIMETER.	You go and do what you men know you need to do. I will wait here.
JACK.	We don't even know where we are. What if you sail off while we're helping McBride.
PERIMETER.	You have my word. I will not leave without you or without word from you.
RICK.	Without word from us?
MCBRIDE.	Come on. Sophie!

Rick and Jack follow McBride, all calling out for "Sophie."

RICK.	I wonder how long we were out?
JACK.	I'm not sure, but it was a while. I don't feel well myself.
MCBRIDE.	I'm sure we were asleep for quite a while—to get us to this place. (*Beat*) What am I doing? (*He stops.*) Look at this. Here we are in the middle of the night. We don't know where we are. We were on a ship and were somehow put to sleep. And here I am looking for someone, from something I don't know if I can even find.
RICK.	McBride . . .
MCBRIDE.	And on tops of that, I've dragged you two along. What's wrong with me?
JACK.	We chose to be here.

MCBRIDE.	I'm confused. I'm angry. I'm hungry. I'm thirsty. And I'm . . .

They stop. In front of them is a large rock. On it is spread out fruits, breads, and drink.

RICK.	What's that?
JACK.	Is that food?
MCBRIDE.	Out here in the middle of nowhere? (*He looks around.*)
RICK.	Fruit. Bread. Water? I just don't know . . .
MCBRIDE.	This isn't right.
JACK.	No, it's not, but I *am* hungry.
RICK.	Maybe a little, just a bite or two.
MCBRIDE.	It is tempting.
RICK.	(*Grabbing some water and drinking it)* Yes. Man.
JACK.	(*Hesitantly taking a piece of fruit and taking a bite*) That *is* good.
IDIZOMARZA's VOICE:	Take. Eat. Drink.
MCBRIDE.	Idizomarza!

She steps out of the shadows.

IDIZOMARZA.	Julian McBride Anderson.
MCBRIDE.	What going on? Why have you brought me here.
IDIZOMARZA.	We can talk. You need food and drink.
MCBRIDE.	I need answers.
IDIZOMARZA.	Rick Eugene Billingsley, drink more. Go on. Jack Fitzgerald Kennedy, eat the fruit. Keep going.

RICK.	This is so good. Thanks, Idizomarza.
MCBRIDE.	*(Realizing that something is wrong)* What?
JACK.	*(Sitting down to relax while eating)* This fruit is so delicious. And this place: it's just paradise. Look.
RICK.	I know. *(sitting near Jack)* I love it. It's so peaceful. I could stay here forever. Build a little shack over there.
JACK.	I can see that.
MCBRIDE.	*(to Idizomarza)* What have you done? *(Goes to the men and hits the food and drink out of their hands.)*
JACK.	*(Standing up angrily)* What are you doing?
RICK.	*(Angry)* What's your problem?
MCBRIDE.	It's poisoned. She's poisoned you with the food and drink.
RICK.	You're paranoid, McBride.
JACK.	Don't be ridiculous. *(Grabs another piece of fruit)*
MCBRIDE.	What are you doing?
IDIZOMARZA.	Perhaps your friends would like to settle here and enjoy life, give up your little search?
RICK.	She's right, McBride. It's a hopeless cause. This place is great. Look around. The sun's starting to come up. This could the greatest place on earth. I could live here.
MCBRIDE.	You have a wife and daughters.
RICK.	*(Thinking)* They'll be all right. Caroline's smart. She can raise the girls.
JACK.	Good thinking, Rick!
MRBRIDE.	And you are a Congressman!

JACK.	They're all crooked. They can keep the seat. I'll stay here.
IDIZOMARZA.	See. Join them, Julian McBride Anderson. Eat. Be as content as they are.
MCBRIDE.	No.
RICK.	Come on, McBride. It's great. You know you're hungry.
IDIZOMARZA.	You know you are hungry.
MCBRIDE.	What have you done? Why are you doing this?
IDIZOMARZA.	Give up your search.
MCBRIDE.	Why? I can't.
IDIZOMARZA.	Give up your search. Join your Lotus-Eaters.
MCBRIDE.	You must think me weak and shallow. I'm afraid that you've misjudged me.
IDIZOMARZA.	On the contrary, I fear you are more stubborn that your very life can bear.
RICK.	I think I'm going to take another nap.
JACK.	I think I'll join you.

They doze together.

IDIZOMARZA.	Join your friends.
MCBRIDE.	Never. (*Beat*) Where is she?
IDIZOMARZA.	I warned you. I warned you with all my might. And still you followed. I warned you to stop, to let things be.
MCBRIDE.	Where is she? (*pause*) Is she alive?
IDIZOMARZA.	A sensible question! Finally? And I shouldn't answer it. I was asked not to answer it . . .

MCBRIDE.   Asked . . .?

IDIZOMARZA.   But I do respect your determination, so yes, I'll
                    answer you. Yes, she is very much alive.

MCBRIDE.   And is she . . .

IDIZOMARZA.   That's all I'll answer! I shouldn't have answered that
                    one!

MCBRIDE.   But you're some sort of . . . I don't know what you
                    are.

IDIZOMARZA.   For whatever I am, Julian McBride Anderson, I'm still
                    a human being. That's why I answered your question.

Male screams come from off-stage.

MCBRIDE.   (*Running to the edge of the stage*) What's that?

IDIZOMARZA.   (*Walks up to join McBride in looking*) I was not aware
                    of this.

A sound of a gunshot echoes across the stage. Idizomarza falls to the ground.

McBride rushes to her to check on her. Rick and Jack remain asleep.

MCBRIDE.   Idizomarza!

*A wild man, dressed in clothing suggestive of a clown enters. He is wearing an
eye patch and is carrying a gun as well as a machete covered in blood. He is
dragging behind him a young lady, bound, blindfolded, and gagged. His name is
Polly Hollie Phemus.*

POLLY.   So, that was her name. What a stupid name is that?

Polly points the gun toward McBride.

MCBRIDE.   You shot her! She's barely breathing.

POLLY.   I didn't shoot her enough then. I'll take care of that
                   later.

MCBRIDE.   Who are you?

POLLY.   I am Polly Hollie Phemus. And this is now my island.

MCBRIDE.	What?
POLLY.	I officially claim this island as my own.
MCBRIDE.	Are you crazy?
POLLY.	(*cocking the gun*) Don't EVER call me crazy. I will kill you. In fact, I don't know why I haven't killed you yet. Perhaps you have an interesting face.
MCBRIDE.	What's wrong with you. (*Finally it sinks in that Polly has a young woman with him.*) Wait. (*to the girl*) Sophie?!
POLLY.	(Screaming) Don't talk to her! Her name is not Sophie! Don't talk to her! Or I'll have to do to you what I did to the men on the boat. (*He releases his hostage, who falls to the ground in exhaustion, and then holds up his bloody machete.*)
MCBRIDE.	The men on the boat? What? What boat? Did you arrive here on a boat?
POLLY.	So many questions? What are you, an intellectual, or something? Of course, we came by boat. But I'm not talking about MY boat. I'm talking about the other boat. Yours, I assume?
MCBRIDE.	The men?
POLLY.	Three men. One in a strange tuxedo. I may have to go back and get his cummerbund. I think it would fit.
MCBRIDE.	You killed them?
POLLY.	Of course. Just like I shot your old woman there. And (*noticing Jack and Rick*) oh, just like I'm going to have to kill your other friends.
MCBRIDE.	No, they're sound asleep. They don't even know you're here.
POLLY.	So? What difference does that make? This is my island.

MCBRIDE.	You just got here.
POLLY.	Still this is my island. It's my new home. For me and the love of my life.
MCBRIDE.	The woman you have bound and gagged? The love of your life.
POLLY.	She's mine! She's mine!! If I couldn't get her one way, I found another way.

The bound woman whimpers.

POLLY.	Shut up! Don't whimper. I gave you your chance.
MCBRIDE.	Is she all right?
POLLY.	It's no concern of yours! Now I must kill your friends.
MCBRIDE.	No! Wait. Let them finish their sleep. They're exhausted. Let them have the . . . dignity, yes, the dignity of seeing who takes their lives.
POLLY.	You are an intellectual.
IDIZOMARZA.	(*weak*) Julian Mc . . .
MCBRIDE.	(*goes to Idizomarza*) I'm here. Hold on.
POLLY.	I'll put her out of her misery. (*Aims at her, to shoot her.*)
MCBRIDE.	(*Putting his body in the way*) No! Not yet. No. Let me tend to her.
POLLY.	I want her dead. But, for the time being . . . What did she call you? Julian? Okay, Julian. You look after her while I tie up your sleeping friends. I want them to see me when I kill them.

Polly pulls the girl to a rock or a tree and ties her to it and then takes a rope and ties up Rick and Jack. Meanwhile, McBride is tending to Idizomarza.

MCBRIDE.	Just breathe.
IDIZOMARZA.	McBride. I'm breathing. What has happened?

MCBRIDE.	We're under attack.
IDIZOMARZA.	By an unforeseen enemy.
MCBRIDE.	Aye. This is dangerous.

The sounds of a hurricane rise. We hear the voice of a child: "Momma!" And the voice of a woman: "It's okay, baby. We're okay." McBride is distraught.

MCBRIDE.	Not now!
POLLY.	What are you doing?
MCBRIDE.	Nothin'. Just hearing the sound of the storm.
POLLY.	(*Tying people up*) It's just rain. Get over yourself.
IDIZOMARZA.	You hear the cries? You hear the past?
MCBRIDE.	Always. Aye.
IDIZOMARZA.	Why did you put yourself between me and the gun?
MCBRIDE.	You don't deserve to die and you don't deserve to die like this.
IDIZOMARZA.	The cries. The past.
MCBRIDE.	We're in a situation. I don't have time fret over it now.
IDIZOMARZA.	It's you. The cries are you. You're inviting the sorrow.
MCBRIDE.	What?
IDIZOMARZA.	Don't allow it. Don't permit it. The storm's over. The hurricane is over. Forbid the past, McBride. Forbid it. It you allow it to, the shadows of the past will darken the present. Be strong. Be strong.
MCBRIDE.	But it's there. It's always there.
IDIZOMARZA.	Kill it. Don't allow it. Stop it.

POLLY.	There all good and tight. My sweet Norma is all snug and cozy. You're drunken friends are all tied together.
MCBRIDE.	Drunken? (*having an idea*)
POLLY.	Yeah. All out from liquor and wine. Sleeping the sleep of the guttersnipe. Your old friend here is not going anywhere, even if she makes it though the morning. Now do I kill you?
MCBRIDE.	Me?
POLLY.	Yes. You're a sly one. I don't trust you. Not one bit. Maybe I should shoot you on the spot or slice through you like I did the men on the boat? Or I can tie you up so you can watch what I do to all the rest of the present company, then kill you—mercilessly?
MCBRIDE.	You need me to see what you do?
POLLY.	Need is a strong word. I just met you, but there's something about you. I want, yes, want you to see what the king of this island does to trespassers.
MCBRIDE.	I'll be your witness.
POLLY.	What?
MCBRIDE.	Everyone needs a witness. I'll be your witness.
POLLY.	Why are you so agreeable?
MCBRIDE.	I understand what you're saying. And you need a witness.
POLLY.	(*Thinking about it*) Yes, I do need a witness.
MCBRIDE.	And I will be that.
POLLY.	Willingly?
MCBRIDE.	Willingly.
POLLY.	Even though I'll kill you when I'm finished.

MCBRIDE.	Even though. (*Picks up a container of drink from the table*) Here. Let's drink on it.
POLLY.	What's all this?
MCBRIDE.	A spread of food that Idizomarza prepared for us. It's why my friends are asleep. They drank too much. But let's toast to it. I'll be your witness.
POLLY.	You're crazier than I am.
MCBRIDE.	Drink to it?
POLLY.	(*Grabbing a container of drink*) Drink to it.

Polly drinks but does not notice that McBride only pretends to drink.

POLLY.	It's done. Look at my island. MY island. I am the king.
MCBRIDE.	Your island.
POLLY.	What's the rest of this? Is it any good? I'm starving.
MCBRIDE.	It's breads and fruits and all sorts of foods. It's very good.
POLLY.	I'm the king. I think I'll eat of the bounty!
MCBRIDE.	I'll be your witness.
POLLY.	Funny! (*He starts to eat, enjoying each bite better than the last.*) This is great!
MCBRIDE.	(*Going to Idizomarza*) Idizomarza, are you awake?
IDIZOMARZA.	Hearing every word. Release it, McBride. Release it all.
POLLY.	This bread is the best I've ever tasted.
JACK.	(*waking up*) McBride.
MCBRIDE.	(Rushing to Jack and Rick) Shh.
JACK.	What's going on? Why are we tied up?

MCBRIDE.	Keep quiet. We're being held . . . as prisoners.
JACK.	Is it Idizomarza?
MCBRIDE.	No. She's actually hurt. I'll explain later.
RICK.	(*waking up*) Hey.
MCBRIDE.	No more talking. Our lives are in danger.
POLLY.	(*eating, looking over at McBride*) What's going on over there?
MCBRIDE.	Nothing. Just seeing if they're still breathing.
POLLY.	At least until they wake up! (*Laughs*) You know: it's so beautiful here. So serene. So lovely. (*He goes back to eating.*)
MCBRIDE.	You two have to pretend to be asleep. Trust me.
JACK.	(*Looking over at the girl*) Wait. Who's that?
MCBRIDE.	I'll explain later.
JACK.	Is she hurt? She looks pretty.
MCBRIDE.	Stay asleep!
POLLY.	Are they waking up?
MCBRIDE.	Not yet. (*walks away from Jack and Rick*) They drank quite a bit.
POLLY.	I don't blame them. This is great. Your old woman there puts on quite a table. It's s shame I'm going to have to kill her dead.
MCBRIDE.	What about the girl?
POLLY.	I told you not to talk about her. She's mine. Just because she's starting to make movies she thinks she's too good to talk with people. But I showed her. I won't be ignored. I'm a king. I have lived a life of laughter and crazy, crazy things, but I'm a king now.

And I've brought her here to be my queen. She will love me and respect me. And she'll be my Queen Norma. This place is so beautiful. I had no idea. (*The food and drink are starting to take effect.*) I'll stay here forever. I'll never leave. I may have to leave the woman alive to prepare this food every day. I've never seen anything like this. I've never felt this good. (*He sits down.*) I'm going to have to tie you up in a minute.

MCBRIDE. Why? I'm your witness.

POLLY. True. But you can witness from the ropes. (*Laughs*) After I rest a bit, I'll tie you up. It's so great here. So great. I'm a bit tired. But I need to tie you up. Don't forget: I have guns and knives. I will kill you. But I need to rest a little. Hold on. I'm watching you. I'm your witness, too. (*laughs, falls into slumber*)

MCBRIDE approaches him.

POLLY. (waking up) Hey! Back off. (He points the gun at McBride, who backs off.)

MCBRIDE. I'm not doing anything, just seeing if you're okay.

POLLY. I'm good. Back away. Sit down. Now. I'm just resting for a minute or two before I kill your friends and establish my glorious kingdom. I'll have a castle right over there and a stable over there. And over there, I'll . . . (*he dozes off again.*)

While he is out, Rick and Jack, open their eyes and nod for McBride to untie them. McBride, looking at Polly, shakes his head. He grabs a large limb and approaches the sleeping Polly. As he gets close, Polly wakes up!

POLLY. What are you doing?

Polly starts to get up, dropping his gun, but keeping his machete in his hand.

Before he can stand up, McBride hits him across the face with the limb.

POLLY. (*screaming*) My eye! My eye! (*Holds eye with one hand and the machete with the other.*) What have you done? My eye! You've blinded me!

52

MCBRIDE.   Good.

McBride starts to bring the limb down on Polly again, but Polly blocks it with his with his machete, breaking the limb. The blinded Polly, screaming starts to lunge at McBride with the machete, wherever he thinks he hears him. McBride, knowing Polly can hear, tries to be careful, but with dodging blows, he makes noise. After a struggle, McBride makes his way to the dropped gun and points it at Polly, who stops—as if he can sense the weapon pointed at him.

POLLY.   So, this is it? The witness stages a *coup de tat*
                            against the king.

MCBRIDE.   Call it what you will, but it's over.

POLLY.   Not yet.

Polly lunges at McBride with the machete. McBride shoots him. After he falls, McBride shoots him again. Then after a pause, he shoots him a third time. He then goes over and unties Rick and Jack. Jack rushes to the bound woman.

JACK.   (*removing the gag*) Are you all right?

NORMA.   I don't know.

JACK.   You'll be okay.

RICK.   (*to McBride*) Is he dead?

MCBRIDE.   If he's not, I'll kill him again.

RICK.   What about her?

MCBRIDE.   (*Rushing to Idizomarza*) Are you okay?

IDIZOMARZA.   I'm not well, no. And I'm not going to be.

MCBRIDE.   Nonsense. The fool is dead. We're going to be okay.

IDIZOMARZA.   McBride, I'm shot. And I'm shot pretty well. But you
                            have to listen to me.

RICK.   (*Approaching*) Why did you bring us here?

IDIZOMARZA.   To stop you.

RICK.	To stop us?
IDIZOMARZA.	To stop McBride from seeking Sophie.
RICK.	By bringing us here?
IDIZOMARZA.	Away from everything. To a paradise. To stop your voyage. I tried to stop you, but you wouldn't listen.
MCBRIDE.	I lost Sophie. I couldn't give her up.
IDIZOMARZA.	You never actually HAD her, McBride. Not yet. She wasn't yours yet. And you acted like she was. (*coughing*)
JACK.	Norma's going to need some medical attention. She's suffered a few injuries.
NORMA.	I'll be okay. And if you don't mind, and I know it sounds silly, but please call me Norma Jeane. It doesn't sound right without the Jeane.
JACK.	All right, Norma Jeane.
RICK.	Wait. Are you a model or actress or something? I've seen you before. Is it Lana or Jane or Marilyn?
NORMA.	I'm just Norma Jeane. Just starting out. That's how . . . that, that man found me.
JACK.	Everything's okay now. You're going to be okay.
IDIZOMARZA.	McBride, you saved my life.
MCBRIDE.	I couldn't keep you from getting shot.
IDIZOMARZA.	But you did. The second time. You did.
MCBRIDE.	Aye.
IDIZOMARZA.	Sophie. Sophie. You know, I've known Sophie her whole life.
MCBRIDE.	Where is she, Idizomarza?

IDIZOMARZA.	I actually named her. A good Italian name for Scottish lass. It means "wisdom." Sophie.
RICK.	She's alive?
IDIZOMARZA.	Very much so. Oh, McBride. I promised her mother to keep you away.
MCBRIDE.	What?
IDIZOMARZA.	I promised to keep you from finding her. Her mother has been my friend for life, and when she came to me, told me you were not good enough for her Sophie . . .
MCBRIDE.	What?
IDIZOMARZA.	But it's not just you. That no man is good enough for her Sophie, I respected it. I told her that I'd make sure you never found her, that that beautiful Sophie would always elude you until you finally gave up.
MCBRIDE.	I'll never give up.
IDIZOMARZA.	I know that. Now. And I know you're good, McBride. Don't give up. That sweet girl is alive, and I do believe she loves you.
MCBRIDE. IDIZOMARZA.	I love her with all my heart. But you have to let go of the past. Drop the storms. This is all over. As this day will close, so will its importance. Kill the storms, McBride. I knew your mother.
MCBRIDE.	What?
IDIZOMARZA.	Si. I knew your mother. And I survived that hurricane, too. I was there. I survived it. You survived it. She survived it. It hit hard and then it left. That's life. Some storms take us, though. Your sweet mother, that kind Bonnie is gone, but he lived a good life and she loved you. You cannot dwell on the past. Move on. Go to Sophie. Her mother has just passed as well. She'll need you as much as you need her.
MCBRIDE.	But where is she?

IDIZOMARZA.	Right off the beach, where she promised to meet you. Hoping you'll return. Go home, McBride. Truth lies where you can breathe. Be happy. (*She dies.*)
RICK.	(*Puts his hand on McBride's shoulder*) You have a long trip ahead, my friend.
MCBRIDE.	Aye. But I don't think it'll be quite as tumultuous.
JACK.	What now?
MCBRIDE.	Let's get back to the boat. There are some things I need to tell you before we get there, though. Let's go. Jack, Rick, Norma Jeane. We have to find the authorities and let them know what's happened.

They exit. The lights change in the transition. Transition music plays. The lights come up on a beach where a young woman is sitting, looking out over the ocean. McBride enters.

MCBRIDE.	They say that there's nearly as many drops of water in the ocean as there are stars in the sky.
SOPHIE.	(*Stands up, looks at him, breathes heavily*) Do you believe everything you hear, boy o' mine?
MCBRIDE.	Not anymore.

She rushes to him, grabs him, and kisses him.

MCBRIDE.	Slow down, lass. We've got plenty of time. Some things are better a bit slower pace.
SOPHIE.	You better be here long enough for it.
MCBRIDE.	I'm here to stay. I've found what I need.
SOPHIE.	And there I thought you were missing!
MCBRIDE.	Funny you should say that.
SOPHIE.	You'll have to tell me all about it.
MCBRIDE.	Maybe.

SOPHIE.   Maybe?

MCBRIDE.   Maybe.

SOPHIE.   Hold me, McBride.

MCBRIDE.   Aye. I will. The storm's over.

Lights fade as they hold each other.

Lowery Christopher Collins (Chris) has been an educator and writer for over thirty years. He is currently a professor of English at Panola College in Carthage, Texas. He has taught at the high school, middle school, and elementary school levels and as an English and literature instructor at the college and university level. For several years, he was a high school theatre director and a gifted education consultant. He's been honored with several teaching awards, including the Young Audiences of Northeast Texas Outstanding Service to the Profession Award and the Kennedy Center's Steven Sondheim Award for being one of the most "Inspirational Teachers" in the U.S.

He is also an award-winning playwright of over thirty scripts, a weekly newspaper columnist, a short story writer, a poet, a pianist, a vocalist, a songwriter, a recording artist with Daywind Studios, the founder and artistic director of Stagelands Theatre Company, an aspiring novelist, and a (former) choir director. He's taught a variety of classes, from rhetoric and composition to literature to acting to the Bible.

He holds a Bachelor of Arts Degree in English and History and a Master of Arts Degree in English from Stephen F. Austin State University in Texas and has served on fine arts and gifted education committees as well as on a board of governors for a small playhouse.

In addition to his interests in teaching, directing, and writing, he has a fondness for lighthouses, windmills, filmmaking, salsa, sculpture, Flannery O'Connor, travel, dominos, guacamole, social media, genetics, Maine, landscaping, pillows, gospel music, Shakespeare, marbles, YouTube, quantum physics, movies, weird jokes, maps, trees, cold rooms, and Texas.

He can be reached at mrchriscollins@hotmail.com,

on Facebook at www.facebook.com/tofferdreams,

on Twitter at "tofferdreams,"

and at his website: www.ChristopherCollinsOnline.com.

To view Christopher Collins's books and other writing, visit Ponderlake Publishing, at www.ponderlake.com.

61

www.ingramcontent.com/pod-product-compliance
Lightning Source LLC
Chambersburg PA
CBHW020602130626
46552CB00007B/2998